A Turn for Noah

Susan Remick Topek

pictures by
Sally Springer

KAR-BEN COPIES, INC.   ROCKVILLE, MD

For Joe
and the girls,
Leah, Sara, and Chana
with love,
—S.R.T.

Library of Congress Cataloging-in-Publication Data

Topek, Susan Remick.
    A turn for Noah: a Hanukkah story/Susan Remick Topek: illustrated by Sally Springer.
    p.   cm.
    Summary: Noah has trouble learning to spin the dreidel as his nursery school class celebrates Hanukkah.
    ISBN 0-929371-37-2:   —   ISBN 0-929371-38-0 (pbk.):
    [1. Hanukkah—Fiction.   2. Nursery schools—Fiction.   3. Schools—Fiction.]   I. Springer, Sally, ill. II. Title.
PZ7.T64417Tu   1992
[E]—dc20
                                                    92-22958
                                                        CIP
                                                        AC

Published by KAR-BEN COPIES, INC. Rockville, MD 1-800-4-KARBEN
Printed in the United States of America.

"I can't do it!" cried Noah. "I just can't spin a dreidel!"

"Come on, Noah," urged his friends. "Try again!"
"No!" said Noah. "I can't!" and he walked away.

Noah felt sad. Hanukkah should be fun, especially in nursery school. But things had been going wrong for him all week.

On Monday, when he tried to spin the dreidel, it had fallen over.

And when it was his turn to grate the potatoes for latkes, there weren't any left. He hoped the teacher would pick him to help light the Hanukkah candles, but she chose Leah instead.

"Maybe tomorrow," thought Noah.

On Tuesday, Noah tried to spin the dreidel again, but he just could not make it turn. He did make a picture frame as a gift for his family, but then he spilled the blue paint cup on the floor and had to help the teacher clean it up. Benjy was chosen to light the Hanukkah menorah.

"Today wasn't my day," Noah sighed. "Maybe tomorrow."

Wednesday was not much better. The teacher hid
dreidels in the sand table, and Noah found only one,
while Jessica found five!

He tried and tried, but his fingers could not get the dreidel to spin.

Noah shook his head. "Maybe I'll never do it!"

Then Daniel was chosen to light the candles.

On Thursday, Noah colored and glued a Judah Maccabee puppet and tried not to think about spinning the dreidel.

At snack time, the jelly from his donut dripped on his new shirt. Then Seth was chosen to light the Hanukkah menorah.

Noah stood quietly as the class sang the blessings. Tomorrow was the last day of Hanukkah.

He still couldn't spin a dreidel, and he still hadn't lit the candles.

"Only one more day," Noah thought.

Today was Friday. He decided to try one last time to spin the dreidel. When it slid across the floor, he turned away from his friends. "I can't do it!" he cried.

"Noah," the teacher said, "don't give up! I know a lot has gone wrong this week, but don't give up! Give the dreidel one more try. You can do it!"

The teacher handed the dreidel back to Noah. He took a deep breath. Then he balanced it carefully on its tip, and twisted the handle quickly.

"It's spinning!" shouted Noah.

"You did it! You did it! You made it turn!" cheered his friends.

Noah's teacher gave him a hug.

"Well, Noah. One good turn deserves another," she said. "Today it's your turn to light the candles with me."

As he held tight to the teacher's hand, Noah carefully lit the menorah. His smile was as bright as the Hanukkah lights.